PAIR-IT BOOKS™

Apples
and More Apples

Written by Michael K. Smith

STECK-VAUGHN
COMPANY

A Division of Harcourt Brace & Company

Almost everyone likes apples.

Apples come in many colors.

 3

Apples grow in orchards.

Apples grow in almost every state or province in North America.

Apples grow from seeds.

Apple trees are called saplings when they are young.

Apple trees bloom in late spring.

Apple blossoms are pink and smell like roses.

 9

Apples are ripe in late summer and early fall.

Apples are picked by hand.

 11

Apples are shipped in trucks.

Apples are sold in many different kinds of markets.

Apples are used to make many foods.

Apples make tasty treats.

 15

Apples are even a treat for horses!